Kathryn Lund identifies as a queer, environmentalist, feminist northerner, born and raised in Lancashire and living in Yorkshire. The death of her mother from bile duct cancer and her own functional neurological disorder with its associated mental health problems are strong influences in her writing.

She graduated her MA with a distinction and the Blackwell Prize in creative writing. Her first novel, which was developed from her major project, is due to be published by Atmosphere Press and is titled *The Things We Left Sleeping.*

For Grainne, Maeve, Sophie and Jim.

Kathryn Lund

THE THINGS WE KEEP IN THE CUPBOARD

A Collection of Short Stories

AUSTIN MACAULEY PUBLISHERS™
LONDON • CAMBRIDGE • NEW YORK • SHARJAH

Copyright © Kathryn Lund 2022

The right of Kathryn Lund to be identified as author of this work has been asserted by the author in accordance with section 77 and 78 of the Copyright, Designs and Patents Act 1988.

All rights reserved. No part of this publication may be reproduced, stored in a retrieval system, or transmitted in any form or by any means, electronic, mechanical, photocopying, recording, or otherwise, without the prior permission of the publishers.

Any person who commits any unauthorised act in relation to this publication may be liable to criminal prosecution and civil claims for damages.

This is a work of fiction. Names, characters, businesses, places, events, locales, and incidents are either the products of the author's imagination or used in a fictitious manner. Any resemblance to actual persons, living or dead, or actual events is purely coincidental.

A CIP catalogue record for this title is available from the British Library.

ISBN 9781398432758 (Paperback)
ISBN 9781398432765 (ePub e-book)

www.austinmacauley.com

First Published 2022
Austin Macauley Publishers Ltd®
1 Canada Square
Canary Wharf
London
E14 5AA

Table of Contents

Whatever Happened to Sarah-Jayne?	**9**
Transplant	**29**
I Salute the Sea	**47**
The Things We Keep in the Cupboard	**69**

Whatever Happened to Sarah-Jayne?

One Tile

Orson's desk was in Orson's office. Orson's office consisted of:

Orson's computer.

Orson's un-killable pot plant.

Orson's posture-support execu-chair.

Orson's walls.

There were eight-and three-quarter blue worn carpet tiles, one door, one window, one view of the road. And one view of the sign for Purified Petra-Chemico Research Appliances Break-Out Division Co.

Orson was not sure what Purified Petra-Chemico Research Appliances Break-Out Division Co. did, but he did it. For 15 years now, at his desk with the un-killable pot plant and the carpet tiles. He was doing it then, as he did what everyone does at work, which is play online and google a little light porn.

Then it happened.

Orson's office—neat, tidy, smudged with a dirty film of traffic from the motorway below, went away. A white, painfully empty corridor appeared in its place. Orson's desk was in the middle of it. Orson was at the desk.

That was all, absolutely nothing else happened to Orson.

It was after a pause, when perhaps moved by some change

in the quality of light, or maybe in the silence, Orson looked up. He saw the corridor, saw the long white walls, the outlines of doors. He had a thought, which was different than the one you or I might have in that moment. It was finally, *finally*.

Then Orson did what he always did whenever anything happened. He continued sitting at his desk. Time might have passed, or not. People may have come and gone and moved and existed, banged into his office shouting:

"Hey, Orson."

Or not. Orson did not know. Orson simply continued to sit.

Then something like interest began to show on his round, slackened face. He slid back the posture-support execu-chair. You could hear the sound of it, scratching on the veneer of the silence.

Nothing.

Orson went around the desk. He started a neat, but cautious, little walk into the white space beyond. A corridor, tiles, many doors on either side, stretching on in a big yawn of shape. Orson walked down it. Nothing but walking and doors.

Orson stopped. Looked at a door. It had a sign. The sign read:

The Cloakroom

Orson stood, thought for a moment. There was something about this. This felt…familiar. Like he had opened one door in his head to find another. A door he knew, though then it was bigger, or he was smaller. Yes, that's right. He was small,

he would have to reach right up to touch the handle, strain to try and spell out the letters on the sign:
C L O A
It was over. Orson was sitting at Orson's desk. Orson's desk was in Orson's office. Orson's office closed in with Orson's un-killable pot plant, Orson's posture-support execu-chair, eight-and three-quarter blue worn carpet tiles, one door, one window, one view of the road.

The silence changed again around him, a noisy silence of background that dared him to say it had ever gone away. No one came in, or out. No one said:

"Hey, Orson."

So, Orson did what he always did. He sat at his desk.

He sat there.

Two Tiles

Orson's drive to Purified Petra-Chemico Research Appliances Break-Out Division Co. was 44 and a half minutes. Orson drove it, every day, for one week.

He made the 8:55 coffee with Janette from People Responses. He watched the taught, firm arch of her denier strain up off the floor to reach the sugar caddy. He carried the tray for her.

On Thursday, The Laundress of Leominster went offline. On Friday he spread his hands beneath the table of conference room Alpha Blue and counted the grains of the wood. On the projector, the **'New Five Tier Ethics and Environment for Working Contract'** blurred on screen. The slide changed.

It happened again.

There on the screen, made up of light filters, speckled with dust nodes, Orson could see a room. The room consisted of:

table in country-style pine,

AGA

chintz curtains,

semi-fitted, eclectic units,

neat, untidy Things.

Orson looked at it, confused, unable to work out how this fitted into the new **Five Tier Ethics and Environment for Working Contract**.

On the units, on screen, a cat unfolded. Orson watched the cat. The cat ignored Orson. Still unfolding, it walked, tabby and rather fat. Fell off the edge of the light-picture, landed, rather affronted, in conference room Alpha Blue.

Absolutely nothing happened. No one noticed. No one said:

"Hey Orson, there's this cat."

This time, Orson had exactly the same thought as you or me, which was *insanity*. The cat did what all cats would. Somehow look, to Orson, like falling was intentional, that landing out of projector screens was *dull*. It rolled on the carpet and stretched.

Orson watched the cat. Watched the saunter over, the rubbing of Orson's ankle, the twist around Orson's leg. How it somehow communicated to him, Orson, that all things considered—the universe weighed up, all other options put aside—it was for that moment, Orson's cat. The light-room glowed on screen.

Orson looked at the room, got up.

The cat got up.

Orson walked towards the light-room. The cat walked towards the light-room.

It was in front of him—AGA, chintz curtains, semi-fitted, eclectic Things—all contained inside the plastic of the frame. He had no idea what to do. Finally, the impatient cat head butting his shin, Orson began to heave one leg over the side, a man climbing over the edge of a large paddling pool.

He was in. He was there.

It smelled of them: of scrubbed pine, kitchen table, chintz curtains, eclectic units, AGA, things on the fridge, of hundreds and thousands of days eaten away on those chairs.

It could have been any time outside those windows. Orson had the feeling of still, cut-off February mornings of overnight snow. He had the stretched timeless breath of long summer afternoons when you come in from the sun and felt the cool of shaded rooms. It was all in here.

Orson was in here too. But differently. The weight had gone, here was a lighter Orson. Here was Orson without the polyester mix stretched shirt and in-packet matching tie. Here was Orson without carelessness wrapped round his gut. He looked up. Looked around, curious about what this Orson would see. It wasn't familiar and yet...it was. There was something in here. Something under those hand drawn pictures on the fridge, something under the cat that plumped it up like a cushion as it lounged, tail over the AGA rail. Something under this whole room that teased Orson like a finger through his memory, poking, twisting. Finding a thread:

Marijuana, bad lighting, unwashed skin, awful grunge track played over and over. Blue bandana bleeding into her skin at Glastonbury. All bleeding into one, here. Was she somewhere, here? Orson ran towards the stripped wood door.

His feet were lighter. Dried oranges with cloves hung on the back of the door. Bags for life. Elephants on bell-strung strings. He opened the door.

Impossibly white blinding corridor. Doors leading off on either side. Light, quiet, empty of anyone but Orson.

Orson looked at the door. It had a sign. The sign was a name. Orson knew what it was before he read it. There was only one name it could be. The name read:

Sarah-Jayne

Three Tiles

Orson's drive to Purified Petra-Chemico Research Appliances Break-Out Division Co. was 44 and a half minutes. He travelled it, every day, he watched the 10 denier 8:55 a.m. stretch. He carried the tray, he logged on. He got through Monday, Tuesday, Wednesday. Thursday he walked four times round the waiting room belonging to Trish and sat in her chair.

Trish featured with regularity in the life of Orson, though he didn't count times. He admitted her usefulness. It was some time, after all, since he had last paced the eight and three-quarter blue square carpet tiles which made up his coveted office at Purified Petra-Chemico Research Appliances Break-Out Division Co. He had stopped doing that thing with the lights.

But sat in the waiting room chair, Orson ran out the following dialogue:

Trish: Can you tell me what it looks like in your head, this feeling?

I, Orson: Like a sort of corridor.

Trish: A corridor? Can you tell me about the corridor, or what you are feeling when you think about the corridor?

I, Orson: It's sort of like I've got to walk down it, and there are doors.

Trish: (*listens*)

I, Orson: The doors have things written on them.

Trish: What things?

I, Orson: Things.

Trish: Are these 'things' like the compulsions we've been working on?

I, Orson: Maybe… I don't know…. I think I have to go through them. I have to go up and down the corridor. I have to check.

Trish: Why do you have to do that, Orson?

I, Orson: I don't know.

Trish: You're very safe here, Orson, you know there are no wrong thoughts.

I, Orson. I know.

(a pause)

Trish: You're inside your head, checking things. What have we learned so far about why we do this?

I, Orson: It's about fight or flight.

Trish: (*listens*)

I, Orson: *(giving in)* I know I can't control the universe. I know. It's patterns in my head.

Trish: Do you think that this new pattern, your corridor, is helpful, Orson?

I, Orson: *(lying)* No, I know it's not.

Trish: That's good, Orson. Do you think that you would like to work on your new corridor?

I, Orson: *(lying)* I can give it a go.

Trish: OK then, you're in your corridor. Everything is telling you must walk down the corridor, is that right?

I, Orson: Yes.

Trish: Why?

I, Orson: *(silent)*

Trish: You know how this works, Orson, it's all connected to something. What are you trying to do by walking down the corridor?

I, Orson: I'm...*but how can I, Orson, tell her, when she doesn't understand. About the realness of The Cloakroom, what I told Sarah-Jayne.* I'm...

Orson stopped. Whatever he practised, Orson couldn't explain that the corridor was, well...real. Physical. Not a thing inside his head whilst the world went on outside. Orson saw it. Orson *felt* it. Saw it as he saw his Managers-Must-Have-Motivators Top-Tips Calendar.

Orson stood up, walked four times round again and left. It was seventeen-and-one-quarter minutes back to his Office. Orson clicked the radio all the way back until he cut off the engine and parked.

Four Tiles, Five

Orson's drive home from Purified Petra-Chemico Research Appliances Break-Out Division Co. was 44 and a half minutes. He drove to his flat, reversed. Drove 27 minutes and ten seconds back down the motorway. Parked on the multi-storey in the fifth slot from the end. Remained calm.

It was now Friday. In the foyer, Orson located the layout map, signed in, counted the steps up to his wanted floor. He counted three double flights of ten steps each. This helped him for a while and he hardly had to sit at a desk for long, not really long at all.

The library went on, quietly around him. Absolutely no one paid attention to him. He felt the quietness and the long blank still of the place. He breathed it in and felt his calm.

Then Orson began. There was lots of books. Orson looked at most of them. He pulled them neatly off the shelves with his rather over-large fingers. He pushed them back on. Off and on off and on. This went some time. Only the quickening scrape of book spines half-dragged from shelves, only the sweat clogging between his fingers, only these outwardly spoke of his growing desperation, but it was there.

His breath began to shorten, the slam, slam of books began to quicken to a running stampede along the close packed shelves. Orson felt that horrible slosh inside him as the need to *finish* and the need to *do* battled it out in his stomach grounds.

It happened again.

A librarian appeared. Orson knew it was a librarian because it looked like one. It wore a bow tie and tweed.

The librarian said, "Looking for something?" Orson stood there, looking at the librarian. "Something specific, for something on your mind?"

There was something about that, the way the librarian said it. Like it could read—read the things that wrote across the blank walls of Orson's head. Things like:

Sarah Jayne and the blue bandana / the Cloakroom and what had happened there. Like how he, Orson, should never have told her. How he should have let it all blow away into pot smoke and grass.

The librarian looked at Orson. Orson looked backed.

"This one, I think," said the librarian.

It was a sort of dark pinkish-red. Textured cover. The sort that ruffles goose-bumps if brushed the wrong way. Small. Heavy. On its back. No blurb. Just the cover and on the cover, picked out in blue paint, was the name that Orson knew.

Orson tried to open the book. He could not. Orson tried to shake the book, desperate to see its contents. He could not. It stayed closed, silent, in his hands. He read the front again:

This is the book of Sarah-Jayne

Orson ran. He didn't count stairs. He didn't touch-wood desk-chairs or check doors as he passed.

He ran.

Out of breath. Not a fit man. At the point of collapsing,

hanging onto stairs. Which is when the librarian said, "Looking for something? Something on your mind perhaps?"

The librarian was stood in front of him. It reached out his hands, gave back **This is the Book of Sarah-Jayne**. Orson took hold of it. Orson looked up.

A white, painfully empty corridor appeared in front of Orson. Orson's desk was in the middle of it. Orson was leaning on the desk. His hands were empty. A sort of pinkish-red door with a blue coloured plaque glowed to the side.

The librarian coughed, politely. Orson managed nothing. He was out of breath.

"When you're ready," said the librarian.

"Ready? Ready for what?"

"You tell me."

The librarian perched on Orson's desk. Orson's Managers-Must-Have-Motivators Top-Tips Calendar toppled at the touch of tweed backside. Orson looked around, confused.

"Honestly, Orson, haven't you worked it all out yet? Still, only to be expected. I mean look at you. You're carrying it around like a gutful of slob."

The librarian smiled at Orson. The corridor stretched. Orson felt the face above him grow as empty as the corridor and as strange. Nothing happened. The stretch of the corridor continued, long and pulled out like a spine on a rack. Orson felt what you or I would in those long, heavy weights that passed for seconds, which was uncomfortable. Increasingly skin-pricked and cold, sweat itching in his toes.

Orson turned away and walked towards the pinkish-red door.

The door read:

This Is the Book of Sarah-Jayne

He stopped. Looked at the door, looked back at the librarian who lounged now on the desk, body locked in a cheerful wave.

Orson turned again, back to the door. Tried to open the door. Could not. Shook the door, desperate to see its contents. Could not. Banged on the door, urgent, rattling the handle, heaving his body against its bulk. Could not get through, could only feel it, feel it all in there—the sudden mornings of silent snow, summer swallowed shade, marijuana smoke grown to perfumes, grunge track playing over and over through the background of their days. In there, somewhere, he knew it, *Sarah-Jayne.* Orson pounded the door.

"Honestly Orson, haven't you worked it all out yet? haven't you?"

It was over. The wailing tear of the alarm pulled something apart inside him, starting at his bladder, finishing at his lungs. There was staircases—three flights of them exploding like a logic puzzle above his head—and people. If they knew his name, they would have been saying:

"Hey, Orson."

They were settling instead for other words, shouting:

"Who set the fire alarm off?"

There was the fire-door bar, rattling in Orson's hand.

Orson did what anyone would do now. Orson lost his calm.

Six, Seven, Eight Tiles

In the following week, these are the things that Orson did:
Orson sat at Orson desk.
Orson counted Orson's things.
Orson checked the bad places in his head.
Orson drew the patterns that protected.

Orson counted squares, there were eight-and-three-quarters of them plus one door and one window and 44 and a half minutes to and from this place.

Orson had 8:55 which was People Responses and 9:05 which was Carrying the Tray.

Orson had watching, unstinted by credit card limits, the Laundress of Leominster steam her way through topless sheets and all was well with her, fine with her—she was online throughout the week.

Then, again, it happened. Orson didn't need a change in the quality of the silence to tell him. A white, painfully empty elsewhere, with Orson's desk in the middle of it, Orson standing at the desk.

Enduring, in agony, at his desk.

"You're an idiot, Orse."

Sarah-Jayne. There, in front of him. Cross-legged in tweed and a bow tie, grinning as cream-smug as a cat. Pot smoke curled from her fingers. The smell of unwashed summer, promise, sex. The smell of Sarah-Jayne.

Orson looked up at her. **This is the Book of Sarah-Jayne** lay open across her thighs. She thumbed through, indifferent.

"Bit un-original isn't it? Is this where you shove me, Orse? I mean, please. Can you say obvious?"

The thing that might be Sarah-Jayne took a deep drag, looked at him, rolled her baked little eyes. Such boredom…it had poured out of her, in the end, like a cat with old fish.

"Poor stupid you. I mean, do you really think you can get there this way? You really think that's the way back?"

Her laugh, her horrid little laugh, the way she had done it in the end.

"You don't control the universe you know," she said. That laugh again, her long hair rolling. "Man, that's deep, I may be cooked."

The corridor roared up in front of Orson. There was the throbbing door of pinkish-red. Dried oranges with cloves were hung on the back, bags for life. Elephants on bell-strung strings. Orson was sure of it. Orson was *sure*. He ran to it.

"No, not there. You're an idiot, Orse!"

That wasn't Sarah-Jayne. Some likeness of Sarah-Jayne only. Some Sarah-Jayne-Thing he didn't have to listen to. He ran to the door, pulled on the door, opened the door. It opened this time.

"No, Orse!"

Orson entered through the door.

The kitchen was in front of Orson. This was his house, his kitchen. Orson believed in it. Orson had always believed, known it existed somewhere. Orson had found it, it was here.

All those times he had counted patterns in his head, all those times he had paced the eight and three-quarter blue squares of the coveted office of Purified Petra-Chemico Research Appliances Break-Out Division Co., he had done it to save this. To undo what he had done in the cloak room—and how he had told it to Sarah-Jayne.

He looked around him. On the table a book, light blue cover. Title rough cut, charred out as though by a burn. Shut, on its front. Orson nudged over to it. It read:

What Became of a Boy Called Orson

Orson stopped, looked at the book. Felt…uncertain. The uncertainty grew from his bladder, finished at his lungs.

Orson stood, doing nothing. In his kitchen, getting more and more breathless, feeling strange. Sweat clogged between his fingers, dripped. The horrible feeling sloshed inside him, a wet blackness that found a grip, then started to stick.

Nothing, nothing, in long, stretching time.

He poked, tentatively, at the book. Pulled at the cover of the book. Opened the book.

Water rushed out like a gush of rain across a muddy field. Dirty, brown, stinking of stagnant pits, of clogged-up days. It ran and ran. It ran all over Orson. It spewed out like a flatulent gut. Ran, ran, more water than a book could contain, than a gut or lungs or a body could contain if you pressed it down to its 65 percent water and threw it over Orson. Rotten, choked and dirty, running eventually to rivulets down his legs.

It stopped, leaving only wetness and a blue bandana. Soaking, covered in mud. Orson could see its colours bleeding out. He reached like a man up to elbows down some drain, picked it up, feeling it like he had that last time. He could remember—the mud and Sarah-Jayne.

"I mean, do you really think you can get there this way? You really think that's the way back?" Different voice this time, younger, sweeter. Then her last cry, urgent and without shame..."No, you're an idiot, Orse!"

Orson tried to hold on. Onto the scrubbed table, tea-towel cat, art-work fridge, sun-snow seasons, unwashed memories, blue bandana twisted round his hand. But it was no good. Orson knew. Orson understood. Orson had got it wrong. He sat at the table. He waited it out.

It was over.

Around him Purified Petra-Chemico Research Appliances Break-Out Division Co. materialised. Orson's desk, Orson's office, Orson's un-killable pot plant, Orson's posture-support execu-chair, eight-and-three quarter blue worn carpet tiles, one door, one window, one view of the road. One screen. The screen blinked.

Blinked.

Orson's hands were empty. Orson's gut pushed on the confines of his roll-back execu-chair arms. From below the smudge of dirty traffic, noise wiped itself across the room. Orson sat, watching it grow.

Orson sat, waited it out. One screen, one desk, one view of the road, one traffic smudge, he watched it grow. He had an un-killable plant and he watched noise grow. At 5:03, he drove the 44 and a half minutes home.

Absolutely nothing happened to Orson.

Nothing happened to him at all.

Three Quarter Tiles, the room was whole.

Transplant

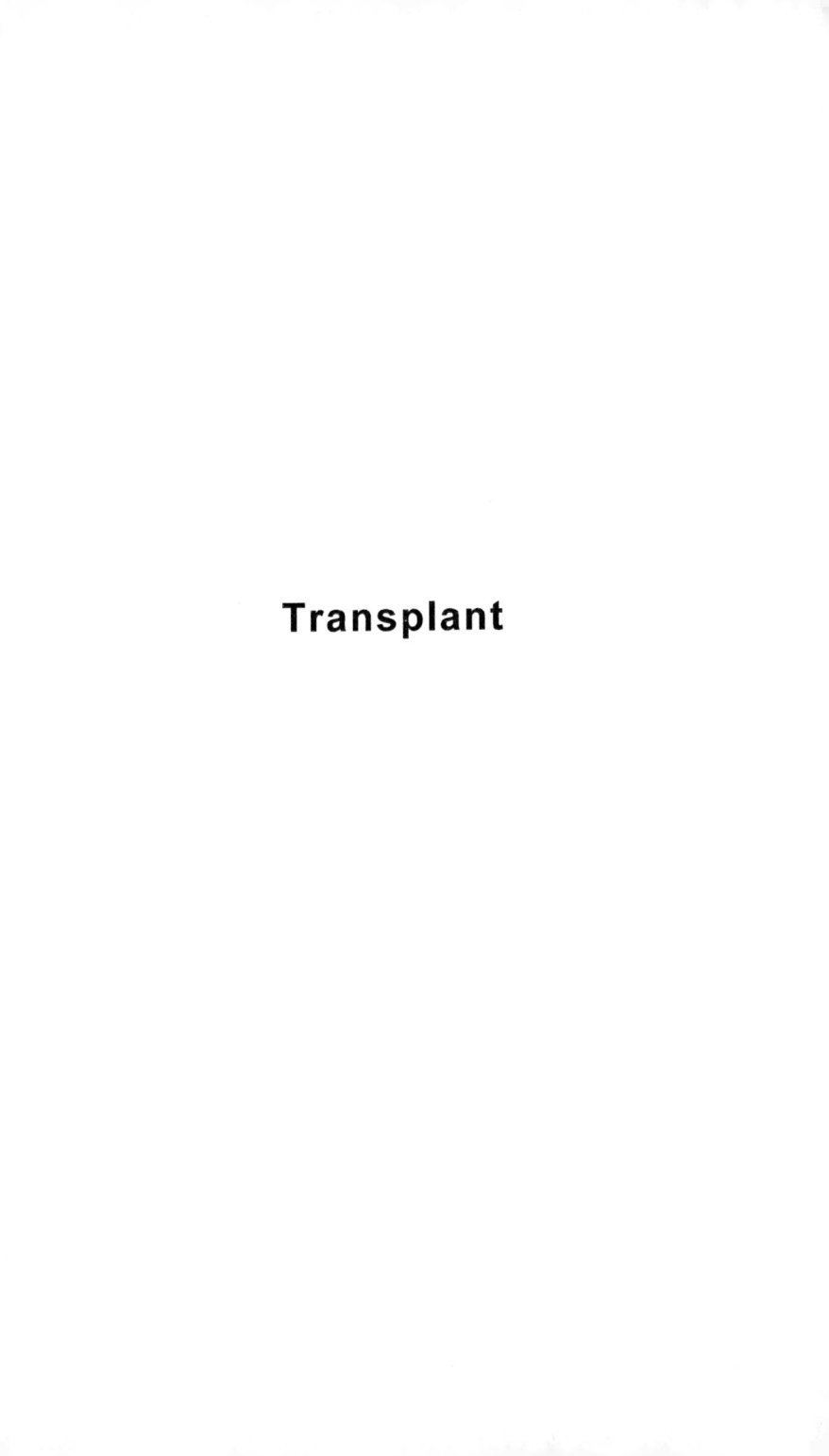

Prologue

This new one had a tendency to run in the rain. I hadn't worn it in yet, it had that new feeling. Baggy where I bent, tight where I lifted. I wasn't sure about the colour, a sort of flushed. Mergatrude told me, it will wear in, in time. It will feel like normal. As though normal was a thing you could pick up again, that you could wear. Feel, this garment is 100% normal. This garment is 100% skin but don't worry. No part of it is made from animals.

I look at it in the mirror. Short. Naked. A little under five foot five. I don't like the colour. I pinch with the hands, it flushes. Short hands, matching the five foot, five inches. I move the hands, watching the blanching fade. I move the hands, watching. Those are brown eyes doing the watching. They have a liquidity, a softness round the edges. A brown of the sort that fades. I open them. I close them.

I open.

I close.

In the darkness I see another body, not 5ft 5. I feel a tall stretch of spine wretch to the end of long limbs.

I open.

Five foot, five inches, runny brown eyes, cold skin. Water dripping off the hair. It hasn't worn in yet. It shocks me, the way it stares back, the way it looks about to run. I watch it. It watches me. Then I move the hand. It moves a hand. Together, we ring out the soaking wet plain-brown hair.

(1)

It is the accepted description that planes touch down. Feeling it do so, Raf Lieke understood that description for the second time in his life. First the planes touch, a rough, brief graze that finds the skin of the earth. Then, if that touch suits them, they come in again for the long slap. All being well, it ends in that plane wheeling, nose first, into bed.

He needed a bed, Raf Lieke.

Four-day blurred and sleep-shaven, smelling of a time zone that he'd lost over the sea. If he'd worn a suit it would be crumpled but what he slept in you could not crease. He wore a yesterday that he'd lost, somewhere over the sea. He tried to rub the out-of-focus time from his eyes and failed. Succeeded only in rubbing in the gassy, plastic-cupped smell of airplane gin.

Ignoring the suck-pressure seal of cabin doors and the inter-tangle press of bodies rising around them, hands grabbed at bags. Overhead spaces dropped over-sized suitcases into the stuffy, over-shared oxygen. Their corners pressed in and caused edged smiles. Raf Lieke remained still, sat in the window, visor pulled down against the glare of the now sky-limited sun.

The window had been rather wasted on Raf Lieke, both trips. He had neither raised it nor lowered it back to see the sky. He had shown, in fact, little visible interest in the thin world of gold-vapour freeze and island cliffs that had streamed their geography outside. Instead, he had treated the visor as you would a drawn-on part of the fuselage. A sketch left by the last, hopeful, passenger as their comment card on experiencing a sealed tube. 12 years between trips had made no difference. Twice in his life Raf Lieke had felt the plane touch. Little had changed—or so he realised when he felt the wheel slap—for him in between.

He had nothing to declare at customs. One suitcase; brown, single brass push buckle for a clasp, string to keep things fastened in. Nothing else came with him. Nothing out, nothing brought back. But then—there was wheel slap, the four days that had driven him, with this suitcase, onto that plane. He had brought those things.

There didn't seem to be a line for declaring those. Well, only one. Raf Lieke took a seat at the trite, desperately atmospheric airport bar and got his whiskey neat, on ice. He sat there a long time, trying to move but every time he tried he felt the plane touch. He felt 12 years drop into the ocean, somewhere in his head, with a great dark splash.

Mergatrude told me, don't live your life in the same places. Not the same cities, not the same doorsteps, not the same thoughts. Nothing they would have done, nowhere that oddly itching coat of skin would be recognised. That's the agreement.

That's the agreement that we made. Stick to it.

(2)

Raf Lieke didn't start his journey on a plane. If you were to go fishing in the ocean, perhaps off the side of some great net-trawler, perhaps by reversing the plane journey in your mind so that it flies backwards across the sky, sucking in air and time as it goes. If you pulled out that yesterday that he had lost, you would find him somewhere hot and dry. Arid even, where trees have leaves whose edges look like paper cuts. Where leaves remind you only of the sun that burns you, rather than shade.

It doesn't matter where Raf Lieke is in this hot, dripping moment you have saved from the sea. He was never really there, not in his head space. Physically yes, he lived there. Shopped there, slept there, ate there, even had sex there. More often than not with a woman he met over packets of suspiciously cling-filmed meat at the local trade store. But in his head, Raf Lieke just *existed*. In this hot place with the thirsty shade and stony road which cut through the tyres of the toughest feet, no matter how often you walked. You can picture the outside of Raf Lieke there but understand—he isn't there anymore. He never really was.

He is at the airport bar, six whiskeys down. Physically sat there though his body is having a hard time showing it. His shirt is a grubby coastline of sweat-shores littered with debris of body salt and grime. His skin is tanned, still smudging in the orange-sun light of an LED palm, seeking out the warm. A body slightly in another time zone, a mind nearly wholly in drink. Raf Lieke sits there, wondering what the hell to do.

Has two more whiskeys. Touches down. A brief, rough moment, slapping him on the skin. All seems obvious, all seems sunlight and clear to Raf Lieke. You feel the wheels skid, you suspend in the moment of no purchase, bouncing between the graze of force and recoil. You feel it sting all over your skin—clarity. The plane comes down. It either turns for a bed or burns up in carnage and fire. You land or you don't land at all. Clarity, for Raf Lieke.

A bed, or carnage and fire.

A bed for the night.

Her bed. So long between take off and touch downs. 12 years, but to him, little changing in between.

The wheels of the touch down keep skidding for Raf Lieke. They propel him, after mixed calls from the landing tower fail to spot a table and a glass-panel wall, out of the open door. Onto a moving walkway, into a coach which flips and dips and causes him to bury his heads from the lights. Along a road which rolls worse than the coach did. A black-smash surface waving up to meet him, his brown case lagging behind him, his overhead clinking with booze.

Of all the places Raf Lieke had not gone to in his head whilst just *existing,* this was the main one. He hadn't gone here, smelt here, slept here. Not her blue front door, not her cherry-berry reed-sticks, not her New York skyline bedspread with tea stain over the docks. He hadn't gone here, to her. Not outside of his head. Now he was here. Physically on the doorstep, underneath the cherry-berry tree, smelling the bark.

Raf Lieke plunged, suddenly very cold and sick. He wondered if this was carnage. He wondered if this was landing, or oblivion.

Mergatrude, he picks them specially. Hobbies, interest, appearance. Shampoo brands. There is no overlap. Nothing. Nothing that connects you to them. Nothing that is the same. Don't go there, to where they existed, don't live your life in the same places, that's the agreement. I agreed. I have to confess I didn't really think he meant it.

At the time, in that room? Yes, because things Mergatrude

tells you are so real. At the time. In that room.

You should see them. His eyes, the way they look in you. The feel of his voice around you in the air. It's soft you see. It's so soft and then he's grabbed you. There's no way out. You believe. In that room, with his eyes in you, you believe.

I was a believer. I agreed.

(3)

Landing had been rough on Raf Lieke. He'd never expected a welcome party, but somewhere in that head a placard with his name on it hung hopefully on a cherry-tree, a strange bare-branch waving in the scratchy palms.

The house was dark, she wasn't there.

12 years—feeling like longer sometimes in between—why shouldn't she have moved? Why should she have lived in some sort of static? A plane forever suspending above a New York skyline, circling in an air freshener renewed by cherry trees and her shampooed hair after sex.

Raf Lieke thought about sex. He thought about knocking on the door and having sex with the flats new occupant as a sort of substitution, a plain one for one swop. He thought about a grin over the meat fridge, the unreadable labels and the offer to cook that had never been more than the smell of pretence caught in the bottom of a burned-out pot.

He dismissed the smile and thought about the world behind the door. He thought about that body—her body—always so easily cold, wrapped in the Statue of Liberty bedspread, a head poking out on top where they should be the crown.

He thought about that. Raf Lieke thought about that a lot,

from in that doorway.

I did see it, beforehand. Only her face. The rest was covered over with a medical sheet, folded back at the breast where they'd pulled over the spare bit of cloth. I could see her breasts weren't big. Felt bad, for thinking that. Could see she had a fringe. Hated fringes too, wondered if she'd liked it. Must have, to have kept it so neat, so tidy.

Brown hair, with a fringe cut.

It was ages since I'd had a haircut. People think they make you better, things like that but they don't. It was a long time since I'd cared about such things. It was a long time since I'd cared about much at all. Until Mergatrude.

Then, I hadn't believed him.

Then, there she was on the medical slab. Brown hair, with a fringe cut. Smaller than me. A bit dumpy, about five foot five. But healthy. That's the thing. They have to be healthy when they go. There has to be nothing wrong with them at all. Nothing wrong and nothing at all to connect you. No way at all that your lives have ever crossed.

Then you have to be willing to let your life go too. All of it. Not a single part comes with you. That's the price you pay. It's not a lot.

I'd thought it wasn't a lot, sat there with Mergatrude. In that room, his soft voice on me. All the pills, all the meds, all the scans, all the prodding, all the poking. All the therapists, the occupational-ists, the self-help-ists, false-hope-ists, all the pain that twisted out the sky. I'd thought about it. What I swallowed every single day. Then about Mergatrude. What he said. What he promised. To take it all away. He promised.

When you have nothing left, you have Mergatrude. When

you've taken all there is to take, he gives you something back.
He gives you the ultimate thing.
  He gives you a chance.
  What price wouldn't you pay for that?

(4)

It is the accepted description that things do not just happen. Take Raf Lieke. Stimulated to travel oceans, breach years, he finds the voice he hoped to hear from the landing tower has moved on. Radio waves severed, her chair occupied by strangers who call in their own friends on frequencies Raf never tuned into, static in his ears. He was lonely. Hungry, feeling like a sock puppet somebody picked up and worn. Then worn and worn.

Picking up his brown suitcase he turns, unsure once again what the hell to do now it comes down to it. It is hardly surprising that, having failed to exchange any of his currency (he paid at the bar by the wonder of plastic) he begins an aimless, watery-sun-drop walk. Down the road, for the road is sloping. Along, along. It is getting late; he has to go somewhere. Buses pass him, lighting up with routes that show that 12 years has left them determined not to change. Chesterfields, Brierlygate. Heyn, via Wayton.

Wayton. That makes him pause. Think a bit. The sun drops right away as he does so. The mouth guards of the shops wind down, speaking only graffiti. Everyone with somewhere to go walks past.

She walks past.

He could have sworn it. He could have rolled down his mouth and given it his best graffiti. She walked right past, brown hair blossoming, on the other side of the road.

Her walk was strange, like she was trying to take a longer stride than her legs could reach. But he was sure...

That's Raf Lieke. Thinking that because he went to an address he knew once, because he walked the main road from it, because he stood by a bus route he used to take, that somehow, somehow, the universe had fate.

As though other people don't have logical reasons for going to places.

As though there aren't only so many places in the world after all.

It was cutting her fringe. That was the first big mistake. When I got out and moved on I thought I would make it mine by changing the hair. Me outside, me inside, I would make us match. But that body was right. That fringe—it suited the face. I'd cut it.

Big, big mistake. Really, big one.

Raf Lieke was the next.

(5)

The most romantic of love stories hinge on set propositions. Any airport lounge novel will show you this. Under the lurid covers and embossed jacket fronts you will find again and again that love will triumph, that love will stave off disaster, that love will fight the evil mechanisms of plotters and that which seeks to derail it. That love will, no matter what the disguise, see through and know its own, saving all with a kiss.

Raf Lieke, stood on the street, his purple orchid and

Havana leaf shirt beginning to stick as the rain attacked the tidelines of his skin. He felt the narrative of his love story engulf him, saw it walk past on the other pavement, walking funny, wearing a mac. 12 years, it was nothing. This was the moment. This was clarity. This was hard feet finally off a stony road, this was her. Brown hair, fringe, short, not more than five foot five, but man she moved it, moved it like jazz, even when she was walking. She was the reason he learnt that time to dance, in the Blue-Rio Bar with its trumpets on smoke-setting and it's sweated out notes and her skin pinching up under his hands, flush-pink. She was the reason, absolutely, for it all. For the years that followed in countries of cheap-bar suns and the burn of LED palms that gave no shade.

That new, odd stride, couldn't hide it. She smoked in the rain, she steamed.

She was the reason he ran now across the road. Raf Lieke, going all out for conventions of the genre, not caring about the bus, or the rain or anything else that got in his way. His brown suitcase abandoned, his arms flapping comically. Raf Lieke, finally starting to catch up, his breath left somewhere behind.

He called her name. Called again as she didn't turn. Ran in front of her, stopped her, dead. He looked at her, Raf Lieke, seeing again those brown eyes. Confusion swamped there, full of liquid. They opened, they closed. They watched Raf Lieke who stood, suspended, unsure now he had achieved his moment what it was he was meant to do.

Then he touched her hair.

It had shocked me, the rain—the way this body moved when it felt the rain, it shocked me. It had a tendency to run, to suddenly burst out running in the rain.

And dance. And dance.

That is how I found out it danced, there on the street in the rain. He reached out and touched the hair, then the hands. The hips moved, like a response, I had no control over them. I felt his hands, Raf Lieke. I didn't know his name then, I didn't know him but he knew this body, he called it a name. Her name. Her, who had cut this fringe before me, who knew this body danced before me, who had run with this body before me, through the rain.

And it turns out I like dancing.

How far wouldn't you carry a lie, to go on dancing? It's not hard to cross the road, read a suitcase label. Not hard to smile and invite him home, through the rain.

How far wouldn't you go? Haven't you ever danced through the rain?

(6)

When entering a strange flat—or the flat of someone not seen in a while—there are certain social conventions that have to be observed. It's inevitable. Raf Lieke does not deviate. He answers yes to a tea/coffee/beer. Whichever one is got from the white painted kitchen with its nested rainbow espresso stack and four ceramic plates of the Scottish lakes.

Raf Lieke looks around, uncertain, wondering which of the chairs he should take to sit down. The high backed bright exploded orange. The deep burrowing cream thing, both of them smelling of new. He observes that she's changed.

Mainly in outward taste. She had got—random. Classy in some things, but others? A red bus coin tin, a pottery monk milk-jug with arm handle on its side? A jam-pot donkey? They seem odd to Raf Lieke. Not what the Statue of Liberty should keep in her folds.

Differences also in her outward action. How she sat sideways, hooking knees over the arms of the chair. Not using a coaster, putting tea/beer/coffee straight down on the top. Different clothes. 12 years.

Raf Lieke has nothing to say. He'd loved her. Loved cherry-berry, New York sky, her pale skin, the colour flood under his hands when he'd held on, her brown eyes open in the dark, her brown eyes shut. Her brown eyes shut, under him in the dark. He loved her.

Coconut. This flat smelt of coconut, of candles on the side that were nutty and dark. Her pale skin, Raf Lieke thought of it, of what she'd felt like when she flushed like a bright sun in the sheets and the dark.

There are conventions. She seemed happy to forgo them, but nervously. It was rather shockingly like a first time. For her, with her nervousness and the pain under red-flower-head sheets in the in the dark. Raf Lieke didn't notice. Not the pain part. Who wasn't nervous after 12 years and after 12 years— or so he found, once there was touch down—nothing very much had changed for him at all.

Mergatrude told me. Not the same cities, not the same doorsteps, not the same thoughts. Don't go there. It was an agreement. But then, I did what I did.

I don't suppose I will have long. Not until Mergatrude finds me. But it is a better not long than before. It is a not long with colour in it. With choices.

Raf Lieke was choices. Bad choices maybe but made

choices all the same. I prefer to think of it as a scientific choice, or, if you do not like the sciences, a human choice. What human after all, wouldn't want to know? Know if she loved Raf Lieke. Would have taken him back, would have let him into bed? Would she have liked it once again when he kissed her here...here...here.

Raf Lieke. This body remembers you. This body remembers you very well. It's a human experiment. I can't help but want to know.

This body knows.

I open the eyes, I close them.

I close them. It is easier to be one body when we are in the dark.

(7)

Humans. They are programmed for intimacy even when they are trying to avoid it. Look at one-night stands; the most basic need for contact, the fundamental need to touch another human form. Bound by common behaviour, achieving what none of the group want at all—intimacy. Humans. They don't always realise what they do.

Raf Lieke thought he knew. What he did, what he had in life. It was right there in front of him, wrapped these days in red-head-flowers, a girl under a wild-meadow sheet. Red heads on white. That was right; it suited her, according to Raf Lieke.

He was naked now; a long exchange of sleep cycles wrung out through the washer and dried on jet-trails in a powdery sky. She wasn't sleeping. Brown eyes were open on the pillow under the fresh cut fringe. Brown hair was in his fingers, sticky from sweating. She was looking up at him. Flushing and annoyed.

He had asked her, about changing back to the old shampoo. Raf Lieke, his fingers searching with longing in her hair. It had upset her; she had rolled away from him.

You're a man—you like eyes and hair—and bodies.

"What should I like?" he replies, cross in his confusion. He rolls her back over, skin flushing under the press of his fingers. Those brown eyes, staring.

What you see inside.

"You're inside," he says, fingers still pressing.

Staring.

Yes... yes. I am

She waited silently until Raf Lieke had no choice but to release the pressure of his fingers and watch as she rolled away.

I didn't believe Mergatrude and now, now I think it is all too late. I broke the agreement. I couldn't help it. I need someone to know that, even though there is no one to tell. I opened those brown eyes, I cut that fringe, I felt from those short legs always a message to run in the outbursts from rain. How fast, brilliantly fast this body moves in the rain.

It likes jazz, it moves to odd-ball beats. It surprised me with the things it knew—and then, then I couldn't help it. I really, really had to run in the rain.

Mergatrude. I broke the agreement. I do not expect that I have long. A not long with colour at least. He has given me that, for all I have disobeyed him. He has given me that, for all I am about to pay the price.

I am not going to be frightened, to pay that price. I see it as a choice, of what I did with it. Singing, dancing, making love under bedclothes. Opening your eyes without screaming at the light.

A chance.

What wouldn't anybody pay for that?

(8)

Things come to an end but they are rarely over. They continue on into the afterwards, a line that blurs into the litmus paper, bleeding out until the colour runs dry. Raf Lieke, making for an ending at the airport, has plenty of lines to follow, mainly ones marked on the floor in tape, or outlined for him on the swinging overhead signs.

He has nothing to declare at security. Nothing to take with him, nothing he wants to bring back. Raf Lieke heaves his suitcase to departures. Joins the line all people join in these times. Has his whiskey sweet with coke to preserve his breath when he gets on the plane.

Has four, crumpling face at the mixer like a neat man will. His clothes are mixed too, half straight-up, half rough outlines that look about ready to go.

Raf Lieke steps down. Manages the door this time. The boards light up with destinations, though only in their graphics have 12 years shown any sort of change. Raf Lieke, with his brown suitcase and his yesterdays going with him again.

Raf Lieke, getting on the plane.

Window seat, but it is wasted on him. For the third take off of his life, he ignores the instruction of the stewardess to slide the visor up. To see the un-peeling slap of the tarmac become the blood rush of the rose and ice-form sky. It was a long peel, that runway. It was a long peel of skin that tore itself from Raf with every skid of wheel. It caught underneath and dragged away his flesh in the long rip of the disconnecting shade.

Then there were only the gold-freeze vapours, the threads of sky-clear streaming their way past him on the plane.

If you were to watch him—perhaps by playing out that plane ride in your head so that air and time flew out of it, like the white trails that float behind it in the blue—you might see, somewhere over the ocean, something happen. Something fall out of the fuselage. Not a single thing but a single thing made up of singular things. Like a red bus coin tin, a jam pot donkey, a pottery monk milk-jug with arm handle on its side. Like a flower meadow, opening outwards as it falls.

Falling, with yesterdays, right downwards into the tide.

In the far-below surf, cherry blossoms drift amongst the wreck of New York, floating by The Statue of Liberty, headless, on its side.

Raf Lieke, looking for somewhere to land.

What wouldn't any body pay?
I don't fight, I don't resist. It was borrowed, all of it. I give it back. I pay the price.
I open my eyes to the bright white sky and it is nothing but flesh and muscle. It's a body with no content, no memory at all.
But, Lord, how it dances.

I Salute the Sea

Reboot System Error

There is no sound yet but they are loading it.

I can see the buffer symbol in the air above the road. I turn to look at her. She is the real thing. Her hair a grey hank, her face a colourless collapse of skin that has never known the light. Real skin, real eyes. I look at her. I manage to move my hand and shift it to where skin shows through the slit in the gown.

"No touching."

A real voice.

Not her voice, a voice coming out of the dark of the walls. Not our voices, the buffer is still loading, we have no voices yet. In there, in the picture, that is where I will hear her. Or, at least, the voice they choose for her. What will she sound like? What will I? I feel what must be muscle move in my throat. I want to speak to her, I want so much, for her to hear my voice.

It still won't load and the picture is jerking.

The road and the sky and the buffer all slip. The picture gone there is nothing but the dark room which we both sit in. Our two chairs, the air vents. I feel a bump like something has dropped through my body, the air lifts my leg hairs, I feel them. The muscle in my throat moves again and I swallow. Swallow. It is liquid—spit. My tongue pushes out to my lips and I feel her. Her breath, warm breath, from the chair where she sits.

Something moves even lower down in me and I am glad, for a second, of the dark.

It still won't load.

Loud sounds, footsteps and low voices, knock a way into my ears. There are people there, in the black of the room around us. People who can move legs, arms, lips. I hear them, talking, moving. A light explodes and shrinks to a pinpoint and the noise moves round again.

"It's another fucking connecter gone..."

"Hand me that..."

"Shit, look at this crud."

Something in me hurts. It's a dread all the lights will come on—all the lights will come on and the doors will open and the trolleys wheel in to take us away. We will see each other only as we are here. I'll never get to tell her how I dream about her voice.

"Clear the room, we're re-loading the program."

A whine like a slapped bone. The room all goes blue. In the chair, beside me she is looking at me. Her mouth does something to its corners. Slow, almost not there. She smiles at me. The blue gets brighter, painful. The black room goes, the picture comes back. My breath quickens, involuntary, free of the regularity of maintained stasis. The picture spreads, all around us, on every wall. On us. Streaming into us. Real, as real as they make it. So real you'd never know. I reach out my hands and grab the wheel. Ahead of me I can smell the promise of the sea.

Error over, Load Disc One

We have taken the car to go down to the sea. We have gone for being young again. She has opened the roof and loaded the sun full of sky. She is alive again, in sunlight. I can feel it on my skin. A warm bone of light worn outside my arm, splintered beneath by the strip of the window frame. It glares silver in the heat. It feel it burn me. There is no sound yet, it is lagging behind the picture. I still can't hear her. The land moves past, blurring, rolling up the scrub and sand. But with no sound there is no feel of it, no feel of movement. No hum of the engine, no taste of air.

I look at her; her mouth moves, red and blood-full. She lifts a hand into the wind and the air splits round it. I see the shape of her laugh and want to hear it.

I want to hear it.

If Error Persists, Consult Manual

It should be enough, to have her here, even in silence. This time is an extra, this is something given to me beyond what was promised. Any reality, anything you ask for, so real you won't know how they make it. That's what they promise, that's what they give you as payoff for that sleep you will never remember, for your sacrifice. And of course you'll get more than one chance at it, of course you will, practically guaranteed.

I didn't believe them when they said that but here I am, my second wakening.

In my nightmares I don't wake up at all. I float inside the stone chasm of my body and chase the silent flashes of her voice.

It's a lottery and one that none of us choose to play. The only choice you have is what contract you sign. All those years before, when I signed, I had no one. I knew that I would be waking alone. Before that first time, there were no nightmares.

Disc One

The buffer drops and I hear it. Not suddenly, not an explosion, but smoothly, invasively, sound is here, speed is here. It was always here and now the car moves. Not things moving around it, not pictures going past, but the car, moving in a landscape that moves green and gold and blue. Air pushes over me, into me, drags though lungs, mouth, over eyes. I taste again, taste speed and movement. The road curves sharp and the wheels bump the sandy dunes and she laughs and laughs and laughs.

If Error Persists, Consult Manual

Alone, that first time they woke me. So sore from the sleep. My toes, far off, stuck with pins and needles that drove in so far they opened my eyes.

"14-74-00-20 awake, inform a transporter."

I sat in that black room, I watched the picture load, alone. It loaded quicker that time, smoother, it was immediate. I picked well, allowed myself the indulgence of going where loneliness would not be noticed, to the places where you would want to be alone. Tested it, in case it was my only chance, with pictures that would survive into the dark sleep—sleep which you lived though, no matter what they said.

Then the pictures had gone, the dark room had come back, the trolley. I had thought that would be all, the only picture I would remember.

Then her trolley was brought in beside mine.

Disc One, Program Running

I twist the wheel and the car swings under me. Her hands fly in the air and she shouts.

"First one to see the sea lives forever!"

Her voice is deep, is a laugh, is the sun-water pouring over the car bonnet and the burning under my forearm as heat makes me an exoskeleton of light.

"First one to see the sea," I promise her, "lives forever."

Are these our voices? Is it mine? Can I remember? Is that what it smells like, the sea, far off, a promise around a next corner, a colour waiting to distinguish from the sky? Can I remember?

I catch her smile; the wind pulls her red curls. Just around the next corner, I hope for it—the promise of a cold, wild sea.

If Error Persists, Consult Manual

I stared at her on the trolley. I couldn't speak to her, I never have, my vocal chords wasted away in atrophy, useless in my throat. She had lain there on her trolley like it was a silence. My head only tilted so far, I could see her head, her shape down to her left hand. Her skin pale like mine from a life under artificial sun.

Perhaps because she felt the stare of me, perhaps for no other reason than it might be a last, snatched chance to move, she tilted her head too.

She looked at me.

Her fingers fought the pull-down of their own weight and lifted. She raised a hand in salute.

Surprised, but without hesitation, I had raised my own back in reply.

Disc One, Program Running

The car sped along.

"You'll see it around the next bend," I promised, sure of what I was offering, terrified it would not be enough. That it would not please her, that she would wish we had gone with her choice when they had wheeled in our trolleys and propped them up into chairs in the dark.

"Oh yeah," her mouth grew wide for me. "Been here before, have you? Cheater."

"How do I cheat?"

Her voice still laughed. The wind still blew round her.

"Because if you have been here before then you know where the sea is. If you see it first you don't get to live forever."

I watched the road run on.

"I'm not sure I want to."

"Not even if you get to live here?"

I looked at how the heat was raising a flush on her chest.

"Maybe," I admitted. "Just maybe."

If Error Persists, Consult Manual

Our fingers had dropped out of the salute. People gathered around. I felt the jolt of the connector in the stem of my brain. I took my chance. What had I to lose, it was a lottery? My words flashed up on my monitor, it hurt, sending them there. It spoke them out loud. Not my voice, nothing like mine, I'm sure.

"Ask her if she wants to wake up with me. If there is a next time, ask her if she'll spend it with me."

Then darkness. It came before I even knew if I hoped.

Disc One, Program Running

"I have been here before, actually."

She turned on her side in her seat and looked at me, fingers bunching a prop underneath her chin.

"Oh yes? What, the last time you woke up?"

"No, though I thought about it. If it was as good as they said, if the program made it as real as they said, then this would test it, coming here. I've been here before you see, in the real world."

I slowed the car, experimenting with the brake pedal, not looking away from her. The road hair-pinned round, dropping downwards through wind bent grass.

"The real world." Her voice weighed the words, cloaked around them like a lozenge. "An actual place, not a fantasy?" Her voice was curious like her eyes, it curled slightly upwards like her mouth. How can a mouth curl up like a question? But hers did. Her voice had a beautiful shape.

"Yes." I smelt the hot sun heating the leather cover of the wheel. I looked ahead, feeling the pull of it, the memory of it. "I've been to the sea, the real one. I went outside."

If Error Persists, Consult Manual

Her picture, her in the dark sleep. You live it, no matter what they say.

Disc One, Program Running

I look at her, her mouth keeps in its shape. She understands me but has no way to know if I lie. She doesn't know me. I turn, look out at the so-real cliffs.

"It was when I was small. Dad got a day pass. It was only for one but he faked it, lied. He said, 'What's the worse they can do to us?' He promised it was worth it. There were these big suits, padded, with helmets. I was much too small but my mum fastened me up inside, it was so heavy dad had to lift me. We went outside…it took ages. All these doors and checks. I thought they would stop us but they didn't, we got outside."

The road hair pinned again, turning us onward.

"And what, what did you see?"

What do I tell her? The waiting in the holding room beforehand, waiting for a week to get used to the light coming in through thick windows. Not understanding, not realising really what was happening but getting it, picking up that this was exciting, this was different. This was something though you couldn't hold onto what it was. Something so good it was frightening. Then those heavy suits, the way both of them held a hand, the way they gripped it so hard it hurt you. So many sets of doors until at last the last one and that wouldn't open, sticking and dad banged it and pulled at it and then – there was outside.

"Trees," I said, my eyes on the cliffs. "There were trees growing up against the door and it was light, it was this strange light, sunlight. Everywhere. And all these shadows from the trees and they all were moving, everything was moving. There was this...this big feeling like something had opened... I can't really explain it. Like something had opened and something inside you had lost the lid."

I feel her hand on my shoulders. I feel my shoulders move down into her touch. Her voice, her lips, on my ear as she talks.

"Were you frightened?"

"Yes. No. Yes while we were waiting but once we were out..." I shake my head, turn around so I can see her. Dad said, 'Take off the suits', Mum was pulling at the straps, throwing them in the bushes. We were meant to keep them on, the uniforms at the door had said so and I panicked. But Dad leaned in and said, 'It's worth it, trust me it's worth it. The life that's ahead of us, we might as well. It's worth it.'

There was this road and we walked along. It was all broken up, bumpy, you could feel things, pressing into your feet, hurting. It felt good and I started to run.

Your feet went up and down and trod on stones, you could feel the sun burn your skin, you felt sweat, it made you want to run, I don't know. I ran and ran and nobody, mum and dad, they didn't stop me. I ran until I threw up..."

I look at her, the hand still wrapping my shoulder.

"I ran until I smelt the sea."

If Error Persists, Consult Manual

The second time I woke up, she was there.

Disc One, Program Running

She sits beside me in the car, touches me. I have let it run to a stop but the breeze continues. Beside us a seagull raises, calling, up the height of the cliffs. Her hands are far away in the black room and on me here, in the car. Her face is still. I don't know what else to do, what else to say to her. I don't know, but I try.

"I wanted to give you a real thing…" My voice breaks off. "I didn't know where else to invite you to come."

I want to look at her, all that copper hair, the sun-flush, the sweat on her cheeks.

She moves in the car seat. I smell her skin. Her hands close up around mine.

"Thank you. Thanks for inviting me." We sit there, holding on. I feel her hands start to uncurl, grip them back, let go, watch her pull her legs up onto the dashboard. She grabs her cotton shoes, tugs them off, her legs fling over the door and she runs, free of the car door, free of the car, throwing the shoes high in the air. They thud into the sand dunes and she laughs, laughs.

"Come on," she calls to me, she turns and waves. "Last one to see the sea, last one…"

I leap out, I run beside her, arms catching her, I feel her, her stomach curve, the heat of her hair. All I breath is her and that far off promise of the sea. It's ahead of us, somewhere. The road goes up and down, is broken up, bumpy. I look up through her hair and around the corner, I see the road go on and on. It is a long way.

She grabs my hand.

We run.

End Program, Switch Off All Users

The real thing. Hair a grey hank, face a colourless collapse of skin and wrinkles that has never known the light. Real skin, real eyes. I look at her. I've never touched her; we've never even spoken. Not in these bodies, not in these voices we signed away long ago.

I tilt my head.

The people gather around again.

That day, that place, that boy who swam in a real sea, that was all I had to offer. I gave it to her. What else was there left?

I feel the jolt of the connector in the stem of my brain. I feel the terror same as the last time only more—because I know, there are no guarantees, none that they will wake you and look, look at what you might lose.

The people move around, I see a part of her through the gap that they make. The side of a gown, a left hand.

Her fingers lift, strain up on the heavy weight, hold up above the sheet.

I lift my own in reply to her.

I salute the sea.

In my dreams, in the sleep they say you will never remember, I hear her laughing. All there is, is her laughing. The shape of her voice wraps around me in the dark and holds on.

The Things We Keep in the Cupboard

* The Last Will and Testament of Linda May Grey:
I leave The Things we Keep in the Cupboard to the girl who comes here after. I leave her the butterfly chrysalis, the man's red wool sweater, two-thirty-three in the afternoon on Tuesday and the other things as listed in the documents I attach. I leave them to her, whole and absolute, to dispose of as directed or as she will. I name those who will see to it my executrix and wish her well with the things that I have left.

Signed by the hand of:

Linda May Grey

* Codex # 1 Butterfly Chrysalis:
I do not want you to be afraid by this. Think of it like the caterpillar. It's always working, that caterpillar. Ugly, half formed but energetic. No one can fault it, it has energy, purpose, it knows what it's going to do. It eats, it grows. That is it. Consumption = achievement. It's not going to be put off course.

That caterpillar—she understands.

Maybe not immediately. She's a little blind to begin with, a little over focussed. But then, as she eats away the world, she gets it. The camouflage shrinks and the understanding of the caterpillar grows. What other explanation can there be? There is the caterpillar raw and naked on the branch; there is the understanding. All covering gone, there is nothing left to do but transform.

So, she transforms.

It's not sleep. There in the chrysalis, with nothing else left of the outside world, with nothing else left to devour, she devours herself. All things of that caterpillar go. What emerges is new, transported, an embodiment of that act of consumption. What emerges is destruction on brilliant wings.

It is an act of destruction you see. You must see and understand…you must be careful in those early days, when wings are fragile. When you can so easily step off the thin, cold ledge of the morning and fall.

* Codex # 2 Man's Red Wool Sweater:
note: Item is faded and frayed around the cuffs.

You must take the sweater and go to the house on Shovesbury Gardens. Do not worry about the dogs, they will know you. He will not be expecting you. He will not let you inside. You must persuade him to let you come inside. Ask him to remember the room at the Ravenscott, the dribbling brown shower, the bugs unearthed in the re-used sheets. Sleeping, wrapped in star-light, in the cold of a winter car. He will let you in.

Go in. His house is warm. It smells of dogs and apple wood. You belong there. Sit on the sofa, find a space there. Make an armchair in the front-room of his head, don't ever get up. It is your seat. You must do this. The jumper is yours. I leave it to you.

Do this. The jumper fits you, it belonged to him.

* From the Executrix :

Dear Madam,

I write in reference to the Last Will and Testament of Linda May Grey.

It has been brought to our attention that you have not laid claim to the items entitled 'The Things We Keep in the Cupboard'. Whilst there is no time limit to you laying claim to the above mentioned, may we urge you to do so promptly? Many of these items are, we understand, of a delicate nature and would benefit from prompt reclamation. We would urge you not to hesitate in laying claim to your ownership before any windows of opportunity expire.

Perhaps if you were aware of the exact contents as listed to us by the person named Linda May Grey you may be more willing to come with haste and make your claim. As such, we beg to provide you with this list as entrusted to us:

Item: butterfly chrysalis.

Item: man's red wool sweater.

Item: postcard of Highgate Bridge.

Item: cream summer frock, linen, small blue flower print, size 12.

Item: bicycle, one broken spoke, with basket (wicker).

Item: two-thirty-three in the afternoon, on Tuesday.

Item: pen, paper (sheets of), envelope (one).

Item: the way his chest went up, down, up down, up over the moments of his heart.

With regards for the enduring well-bring of your estate,
This letter is signed:

The Executrix.

* Codex # 3 Postcard of Highgate Bridge:
The Front of The Postcard—showing a picture of the bridge.

For those who cannot see the card, we enclose a description of Highgate bridge from A Guide to Highgate and The Surrounding Countryside, (RRP £ 5.99, net).

Highgate Bridge is situated approximately 15 minutes outside the town of Loxden. Several paths offer spectacular walks to the bridge, most of which are also cycle-ways (see cycle maps and byways, p.4). Highgate Bridge is best approached by foot or cycle for the best view, though it is a road bridge so care should be taken, especially during busy times. It is a known local accident spot.

For the most dynamic view of the bridge, it is recommended that you approach from the east side. Taking the main path from Loxden will bring you through the protected wilderness area which offers a shaded journey for most of the way. The coverage is mainly established native woodland and if you come in the correct season you will see a strong showing of blue-bells and other native flora.

Those who do not wish to cross the bridge can take advantage of the spectacular, if dizzying, views across the gorge from the viewing platform. This is marked clearly on.

(End of extract).

The Back of the Postcard:

Dearest Mary,

15 minutes my backside, more like half-an-hour and uphill all the way. I think the guy that wrote that book may be a sadist. Nathe says it's because I was in the wrong gear but I'm not listening to him since about 9.30 this morning (which is when it was no longer 15 minutes). Everyone's right about the view though.

'It' is getting better. I haven't thought about it as much here. I don't know why. Different places I suppose. Puts it all on hold, means we can come away from ourselves. But I still feel it. Like a river at the bottom of a chasm. Like a really deep gorge.

We can't spend life on holiday. We can't spend life in other places.

I know but wish otherwise and send to you with love from,

Linda May Grey.

* From the Executrix :

Dear Madam,

It is now with some concern that we write to you about the estate of the person named to us as Linda May Grey. The Things We Keep in the Cupboard press with some urgency on us. We beg you to come forward and lay claim to what is yours.

We remind you of our previous correspondence and the time limit which may apply to some of these items entrusted to our care.

With hope as to the reclamation of your rightful estate,
This brief letter is signed:

The Executrix.

* Codex # 4 cream summer frock, linen, small blue flower print, size 12.

* Codex # 5 bicycle, one broken spoke, with basket (wicker)

The dress was a choice, I wore it for both of us, for me and the girl who will come after. I wanted you to take shape from something good. Like the butterfly who takes inside for the transformation all that it needs to be reborn. It will be the pattern of the wings; cream, with periwinkle eyes.

I chose it for a reason. For Mary's stupid river party, with Nathan and the boat. Everyone sun burnt, my arms and chest tanned to the shape of that dress. A whole day in blue and scarlet membrane. I wanted it again, I chose the pattern of my transformation.

I chose the day. Like the caterpillar I felt the knowledge, the instinct, that this day was the one in which I should burst out. I put on the dress. It was hot again, I could have burned again, I had to watch my legs didn't cut up on the broken spoke of the bicycle. You will need to fix that when these things come to you.

I felt the heat-stick tarmac, the linen-cool liquid of the dress. I cycled. I have left you the bicycle so you can return and see. How once you are under the trees it is very shaded. How if you time it right for the seasons, it all turns into a great sea of blue.

* Codex # 6 pen, paper (sheets of), envelope:

These items were used to write the Last Will and Testament of Linda May Grey.

Please see The Executrix for details.

* Codex: # 7 Two-thirty-three in the afternoon, on Tuesday:

This is the moment of the translation, of transformation. I am very confident. I know I have left behind enough of me for success. You will find it all useful, I am sure -

they are very fragile wings but I know you will come out wearing them. I know you will translate with them, ready to truly be.

I understand, you see. It is about destruction. That is the only act that truly passes things on.

* From the Executrix :

Dear Madam,

It is with regret that we must assume that you are somehow incapacitated from laying claim to your inheritance of 'The Things We Keep in the Cupboard'. As previously laid out to you in our correspondence we fear that several of these items will perish if not claimed within a reasonable time frame. We feel it is our responsibility to inform you that we believe that window of reclamation is about to close. We therefore beg and entreat you, come in all haste and take the things that are yours.

If you should fail to do so we shall keep what is left in the cupboard as the unclaimed estate of Linda May Grey.

With regards for the enduring legacy of your estate,

The Executrix.

* Codex # 8 the way his chest went up, down, up down, up over the moments of his heart:

I want you to know it was all about a breath. The house, knowing it was ending. Knowing he was out there somewhere. Knowing I got it wrong. Lying there; the sheets smelling of laundry white, the way his chest went up, down, up, down, up over the moments of his heart.

It was all about a breath. That was the one I took.

I put it in the cupboard. Use it well.